The Journey Within

The Journey Within

Sijeesh V B

CONTENTS

THE JOURNEY WITHIN

Dedicated to Veena, my partner, my first reader, and my constant source of strength.
Thank you for your endless support, patience, and belief in this journey.

1

Homecoming

The Kerala sun showed no mercy; a golden glare that turned the asphalt roads into ribbons of fire. Niranjan parked his car near the Old Bus Stand in Kunnamkulam, his throat parched and mind restless. The vibrant energy of the town contrasted starkly with the ache he carried within.

He had been away for so long, yet the streets felt both familiar and foreign, as though they belonged to a distant chapter of his life.

A lime soda stand caught his eye, its glass bottles stacked haphazardly. The thought of the fizzy tang hitting his tongue made him smile, a rare gesture in recent times. He ordered a soda with salt and sipped it slowly, savoring the simplicity of the moment. As he stood there, memories began to surface, unbidden and vivid.

The bus stand had been the epicenter of his youthful escapades, back when it was a bustling hub of activity. Pazhanji-Kattakambal buses stopped on the right, Thrissur ones on the left. The air had always been filled with the hum of conversations, the aroma of fried snacks, and the occasional sharp honk of a bus. He remembered the magazine shop that displayed rows of colorful covers, the watch repair stall run by Rajan, and the cobbler's corner where intricate leatherwork came to life.

The familiar landmarks were gone, replaced by a sterile new bus stand, yet, fragments of the past lingered in his mind.

He drove slowly toward the church at the edge of the town. It stood tall and majestic, its facade bearing the marks of time and devotion. Festivals here had been grand celebrations, filled with music, lights, and life. Niranjan recalled the church band, its drummer, a charismatic presence at the center of the stage. As a boy, Niranjan had often dreamed of being that man, his hands mimicking the rhythms on imaginary drums.

From a distance, his old house came into view. The walls, once a cheerful shade of blue, were now faded and cracked. The narrow alley that led to it was crowded with houses, a far cry from the open space he remembered. He parked the car and stood for a moment, taking in the sight of his childhood home. This was where he had counted cars as they passed, where he had doodled on walls hidden from view, where his world had once been no bigger than this lane.

"Da, Niranjan!" a voice called out, pulling him back to the present. He turned to see Gopalettan, his childhood neighbour, standing across the road. The years had added creases to his face, but his smile remained unchanged.

"How are you, Gopaletta?" Niranjan asked, stepping forward to greet him.

"Getting by," Gopalettan replied with a laugh. "How's Kannan?"

"He's doing well," Niranjan replied, the mention of his brother stirring a pang of nostalgia.

They walked together to Subrettan's Tea Shop, where the air was thick with the aroma of freshly brewed tea and fried snacks. Niranjan ordered a "Podi Chaya," a strong tea he hadn't tasted in years. As he sipped the familiar brew, a sense of belonging washed over him.

His thoughts drifted to Kriti, his daughter. She had turned eighteen the day before, a milestone he should have celebrated. Instead, he had left her a letter and embarked on this journey. Guilt weighed heavy on his chest, but he knew this was something he needed to do—not for her, not for Poornima, but for himself.

As he sat there, surrounded by the hum of the tea shop and the voices of old acquaintances, Niranjan felt the first stirrings of clarity. He didn't know where this journey would lead him, but for the first time in years, he felt like he was moving toward something meaningful. The road stretched ahead, uncertain but full of possibility.

2

Familiar Ground

The aroma of Subrettan's tea lingered in Niranjan's senses as he walked back to his car. His habit of not rinsing his mouth after a good cup of tea was one of those quirks that reminded him of simpler times. The first sip of the strong "Podi Chaya" had transported him back to his school days, sitting in this very shop, savoring the same brew with friends who had since become strangers.

Driving out of the tea shop's vicinity, Niranjan found himself drawn toward Guruvayur, a town steeped in memories and rituals. The signboards that marked "Guruvayur, 3 km" stirred a mix of nostalgia and longing within him. The town was lively as always, but Niranjan's eyes searched for the familiar, trying to reconnect with a version of himself he had left behind.

He slowed down as he neared the old 'Clock House,' its signature yellow Ajanta clock still standing tall, defying the passage of time. The shop that had always been the landmark, now stood as a relic of constancy amidst the sea of change that had engulfed the town.

Further down the road, Niranjan's car halted near a toddy shop, one that had once been the meeting ground for him and his closest friends. A faint smile crept onto his lips as he remembered their youthful mischieves. This was where he, Sudheesh, and Shinoj had taken their first tentative steps into adulthood, ordering toddy under the guise of religious observance.

The memories were bittersweet. Niranjan recalled the thrill of sneaking out, their nervous laughter as they sipped the drink for the first time, and the scandal at being caught by Sudheesh's father. The humiliation had been palpable, but so was the camaraderie. Those were simpler days, driven by the heady mix of innocence and rebellion.

Sudheesh's face flashed before him—the boy who could make everyone laugh, the star cricketer of their dusty village tournaments. But the laughter faded quickly, replaced by the somber memory of Sudheesh's untimely death. He had taken his own life, unable to cope with a heartbreak that had fractured his spirit. Niranjan had been devastated by the news, grappling with the incomprehensibility of it. Even now, the loss felt raw, a reminder of life's fragility.

He parked his car at a familiar spot and decided to take a short walk through the streets of his youth. The narrow lanes hadn't changed much, though the faces of the passersby were now unfamiliar. He walked past the temple, its walls echoing with chants and the rhythmic clang of bells. The scent of burning camphor and jasmine flowers wafted through the air, pulling him deeper into his memories.

A figure waved to him from across the street. It was Rameshan, a childhood acquaintance who had grown into the owner of a small textile shop.

"Niranjan! It's been years," Rameshan said, his face lighting up with genuine warmth.

"Years indeed," Niranjan replied, shaking his hand firmly. "I was just passing through, thought I'd revisit some old haunts."

Rameshan chuckled. "Old haunts, maybe. But you look like you've been carrying the weight of the world, Niranjan. Sit down, have some tea. Let's talk."

They sat outside a small café, where Niranjan relived the years he had spent away from home, speaking in measured tones about his work, his family, and the decision that had brought him back. Rameshan listened, occasionally interjecting with anecdotes about the people they both knew. It felt grounding, this exchange, as if the past and present were finding a way to coexist.

The road ahead called to him, yet Niranjan lingered for a while longer. He visited the temple, its intricate carvings untouched by time, and lit a lamp in memory of those he had lost. He watched the flame flicker in the evening breeze, steady and unwavering despite its fragility.

As he drove out of Guruvayur, the sun dipped below the horizon, casting long shadows on the road. Niranjan felt a strange sense of closure, as though he had reclaimed a piece of himself left behind in these streets. The journey ahead was still uncertain, but for the first time in years, he felt ready to embrace it.

3

The Unraveling

The ring of Niranjan's phone shattered the contemplative silence in the car. He glanced at the screen. It was Sreejith. Taking a deep breath, he answered.

"Da," Sreejith began, using the familiar Malayalam term for elder brother. "Your wife called me. She's looking for you. Wanted to know if I'd heard from you."

Niranjan remained silent, his fingers gripping the steering wheel tighter. "I told her I didn't know where you were," Sreejith continued. "But she wasn't convinced. Are you sure about this?"

"I'm sure," Niranjan replied, his voice steady but tinged with weariness.
"Where are you now?"
"Guruvayur," he said simply.
"Hmm," Sreejith acknowledged. "Keep me posted. And take care, Niranjan. Whatever it is you're searching for, I hope you find it."
Niranjan nodded and ended the call, his mind swirling with fragmented thoughts.

Everyone had always said he and Poornima were a perfect match. Yet, over the years, their relationship had become a battleground. Poornima's possessiveness and relentless desire for status had drained him. Despite her humble beginnings, she'd always compared their life to others, yearning for what she thought they lacked. No amount of reasoning could convince her otherwise. For years, Niranjan had shouldered her suspicions and criticisms, but it had left him emotionally scarred.

He often found himself withdrawing, escaping into books, meditation, and his solitary walks. This retreat wasn't just physical but emotional. He had fought to stay, for Kriti's sake, but it had taken everything he had. Now that Kriti had turned eighteen, an independence radiating from her, he felt it was time to leave.

A memory surfaced—the first cracks in their relationship. Poornima had accused him of infidelity once, spurred by a trivial interaction with a colleague. Her anger had been volcanic, her words cutting deep.

"What if I do?" Niranjan had snapped in frustration, his patience finally fraying.

The silence that followed his retort was deafening, and for the first time, he saw something shift in her—fear. Fear of losing him, of losing control. But the damage had been done, and though they had reconciled on the surface, the scars lingered.

His thoughts wandered further back, to a time before Poornima, to Aleena. She had been the first girl he had loved, a love so innocent and intense it had consumed him.

Their secret rendezvous at junctions, the stolen glances, the hesitant confessions—it all felt like another lifetime. Aleena's laughter had been his solace, her presence his sanctuary. But life, with its unrelenting pragmatism, had torn them apart. He had never allowed himself to dwell on what could have been, yet, in moments like these, her unsolicited memory.

Niranjan drove aimlessly, the roads winding through green fields and bustling villages. The scenery blurred, but his thoughts sharpened. He pulled over near a small temple, the evening sun casting a golden glow over its walls. The temple bell chimed, its resonance pulling him back to the present.

He stepped out of the car and walked toward the temple's entrance. The scent of incense and flowers greeted him, mingling with the earthy aroma of the damp soil. Inside, devotees sat in prayer, their faces undisturbed and resolute. Niranjan joined them, kneeling on the cool stone floor, his palms pressed together.

For the first time in days, he felt a flicker of peace. It wasn't much, but it was enough to keep him going.

As he walked back to his car, the horizon looked crimson. The road ahead seemed less daunting, and it felt like he was unraveling the knots within, one step at a time.

4

Junction of Hearts

In our village, every kilometer or so, there bloomed a small junction. Each one pulsed with life, a microcosm of our community. A tea shop bubbled with conversation, a tailor stitched stories into cloth, a stationery and grocery shop held the essentials of daily life, and a youth club where the young assembled. In the mornings, before mobile phones imprisoned heads, the news crackled from newspapers, read aloud by eager eyes. Evenings were for sharing stories and laughter, a vibrant tapestry woven from the threads of the day.

One such junction thrived near my house. Shantha, a woman with a warm smile and a sharper mind, presided over the tea shop. Politics, cricket, local gossip—all were dissected and debated within its walls. We, the neighborhood boys, claimed our usual spot every morning, watching the world go by: students on their way to school, the rhythmic clink of lunchboxes becoming a morning song. Among them was Aleena, her laughter like windchimes on a breezy day. She'd walk with a friend, but her eyes, I was certain, always scanned our corner. And so, I, Niranjan, found myself drawn there every morning, not for the chai, but for a glimpse of her.

Months bled into one another before I gathered the courage. One day, with a frantically pounding heart, I blurted, "Aleena, I love you. Do you love me?"

Her reply was a whisper, laced with uncertainty. “I don’t know.”

Deflating. Months of longing culminated in that—a response that hung heavy in the air. Perhaps it was Ameen, her father, a burly man known as Ameen Ikka, whose profession as a loader commanded respect, if not fear. Aleena was the middle child, flanked by two elder sisters and a younger one. Maybe the weight of their futures rested heavily on her shoulders, a responsibility that overshadowed love.◈

Despite the sting of rejection, I remained a fixture at the junction, a teenager clinging to a sliver of hope. Days blurred into weeks, then months. Then, one festive night, while serving food at a temple celebration, our paths crossed again. Under the soft glow of the oil lamps, she adjusted her veil, a fleeting smile gracing her lips. After dinner, as the crowd thinned, I found her waiting by the well.

“I love you too,” she confessed, her voice barely above a murmur. “But I can’t ruin my sisters’ lives. Falling in love with someone outside our community... it would bring shame.”

Her words struck me dumb. Everything else faded—the flickering lamps, the distant chatter—replaced by the sweet echo of her love. As the poet said, the best feeling in life is realizing and being aware that someone is in love with you. That was new to me. Sleep, that night, was a distant visitor.

Dawn arrived, painting the sky in hues of orange and pink. All I craved was another glimpse of her at the junction, a promise hanging between us.

5

A Loveless Disconnect

The phone's shrill ring pierced the tranquility of the car. Niranjan, his heart pounding with apprehension, answered reluctantly. The voice on the other end belonged to Poornima.

"Where are you, Niranjan?" she asked sharply, skipping pleasantries altogether.

"Out with friends," he replied, keeping his tone neutral.

Her response was venomous, laced with a mix of sarcasm and accusation. "Friends? Or someone else?" The question was an arrow aimed at his integrity, a question that no longer surprised him but still stung.

Niranjan swallowed the retort that rose in his throat, forcing a brittle smile for the friends in the car who could hear every word. Shame burned his gut as he realized his private turmoil had once again spilled into the open.

The fight that evening was a replay of countless others—a cycle of mistrust and defensiveness. Poornima's possessiveness wasn't a new development; it had grown with the years, feeding on her insecurities and amplified by Niranjan's increasing silences. She'd demand details about the people he interacted with, the calls he made, the colleagues he met. Every explanation was met with skepticism, her accusations escalating until there was no space left to breathe.

For years, Niranjan had endured this, choosing to appease her for the sake of peace. He'd brush off her words, retreat into his own mind, and focus on providing for the family. But that night, something in him broke. Her relentless suspicion drained the last ounce of patience from his being.

"What if I did?" he snapped, his voice low but cutting. It wasn't an admission; it was defiance, a tired man's desperate attempt to reclaim some semblance of dignity.

The silence on the other end was deafening. For the first time, Niranjan imagined she felt the fear he had lived with—the fear of losing something precious, of losing control. But the moment passed, and guilt flooded his chest.

The memory of their early days together came rushing back—a time when love had softened the edges of their arguments. Poornima had been a fiery force, but her possessiveness was tempered by a genuine affection for him. Over the years, though, the balance had tipped. Her desire for control, for validation through material success, overshadowed the tender moments that had once defined their relationship.

He thought of Kriti, their daughter, and how she'd witnessed their arguments from the shadows of her childhood. She'd grown up in a house where silence often followed anger, where words were wielded as weapons, and where love had become a transaction. Niranjan's decision to stay had been driven by a sense of duty to her. But now, with Kriti turning eighteen, he wondered if staying had been the right choice.

Driving through the city that night, Niranjan found himself drawn toward an empty stretch of road. He pulled over near a small park, its lone streetlamp casting a pool of light on the bench beneath it. Stepping out of the car, he sat down, his thoughts unraveling in the silence.

He wasn't a man who believed in grand gestures or words. For him, love had always been in the small things—a cup of tea placed on Poornima's bedside table without being asked, a textbook he'd bought for Kriti before she even mentioned she needed it. But somewhere along the way, these gestures had lost their meaning, swallowed by the weight of unmet expectations and unaddressed grievances.

Niranjan closed his eyes, the cool night breeze brushing against his face. He thought of Aleena, the girl who had once loved him without demands, without suspicion. Her image flashed before his eyes, not as a comparison but as a reminder of what love could be—simple, unburdened by fear or control.

He stayed there for hours, his mind replaying scenes from the past and the present, searching for clarity. When he finally rose to leave, the sky was beginning to lighten, the first rays of dawn began to illuminate the sky. His heart felt heavy but resolute. He had reached a point of no return, and he knew that the road ahead, though uncertain, was the only one left to take.

6

Honeymoon Haze

Niranjan pulled over near a tea shop on the outskirts of Avinashi, a small town brimming with the simplicity of rural Tamil Nadu. The air was thick with the aroma of freshly fried vadas and strong tea brewed in large aluminum kettles. He stepped out, stretching his legs and calling out to the proprietor. "Anna, oru tea" (Brother, one tea).

The shopkeeper, a cheerful man with a towel draped over his shoulder, responded with a smile. "Vere ethaavathu venamaa?" (Do you need anything else?)◈

"Murukku," Niranjan replied, eyeing the jar of the crispy snack on the counter. As he sipped the tea and nibbled on the murukku, his mind wandered to the honeymoon days with Poornima.◈

Their first long drive together, a road trip to Goa, came flooding back with vivid clarity. It was the first time he had seen her eyes light up with genuine excitement. The journey had been filled with laughter, stolen kisses, and a sense of freedom that felt unshakable. They had stopped at roadside tea stalls like this one, indulging in the simple pleasures of hot chai and crispy snacks. Niranjan smiled at the memory of Poornima insisting they find a "better" place for tea, her youthful exuberance clashing with his laid-back demeanor.◈

"Back then, I thought it was endearing," he murmured to himself, the warmth of the tea mirroring the bittersweet twinge in his heart.�

He remembered her endless stories about her wealthy cousins and their luxurious lifestyles. At the time, her desire to emulate them had seemed harmless, a quirk of her younger self. Niranjan had dismissed it as a phase, attributing it to her being the youngest sibling in a household that often indulged her whims. But that youthful dream of grandeur had grown into an endless pursuit over the years, casting a shadow on the simplicity they once cherished.��

Their honeymoon in Goa was a whirlwind of passion and exploration. They had ventured into the narrow streets of Panaji, sampled seafood at beachside shacks, and marveled at the Portuguese architecture. Poornima had surprised him during those days. Her confidence, her unabashed enjoyment of life, had left him in awe. She was bold, inquisitive, and vibrant; qualities that made her shine in his eyes. Niranjan had thought then that they would grow together, their strengths complementing one another.

But time had a way of eroding those rosy expectations. He thought back to her father's words at their wedding, "We love her very much." Niranjan had interpreted it as a father's protectiveness, but in hindsight, he wondered if it was a warning—a glimpse into the challenges that lay ahead.

The shopkeeper interrupted his reverie. "Ini oru tea venamaa?" (Would you like another tea?)�
Niranjan shook his head, handing over the cash. The man gestured toward a QR code. "Google Pay iruka?" (Do you have Google Pay?)

"Illa," Niranjan replied. He hadn't installed the app on his new phone, a deliberate choice to minimize digital trails during this journey. The absence of notifications, the stillness of his phone, was a rare and cherished relief.

As he got back into his car, he felt a wave of nostalgia and clarity. Those early days with Poornima had been filled with promises. Despite the challenges that followed, there was a time when their love was untainted, their dreams intertwined. As the car rumbled to life and he pulled back onto the highway, Niranjan let the memories fade into the hum of the road. The open journey stretched before him, inviting him to reflect, let go, and move forward.

7

A Glimpse of the Past

Niranjan parked the car near a small junction just outside the bustling town, his heart tingling with nervous anticipation. He checked his watch. Aleena had promised to meet him at 10:30, after dropping her children off at school. The familiarity of her name, even after all these years, stirred something in him—a mixture of excitement, nostalgia, and trepidation.

As he waited, the morning sun cast long, golden streaks across the road. The scent of wet earth and blooming jasmine filled the air, blending with the faint sound of a distant temple bell. And then, he saw her. Aleena emerged from the opposite lane, adjusting her veil as she walked toward him with a grace that felt unchanged by time.

He stepped out of the car, unable to suppress the smile tugging at his lips. "Why are you smiling like that?" she asked, her voice playful, the same tone he remembered from their younger days.

"Just happy to see you," he replied, the sincerity in his voice catching even him by surprise.

He pulled her into a brief, impulsive hug before realizing where they were. She chuckled softly. "It's a road, Niranjan," she teased. He stepped back, awkwardly adjusting his shirt.

“Sorry,” he mumbled, embarrassed but pleased by her smile.

“Shall we find a quieter place?”

She nodded, and they climbed into the car. “There’s a nice café nearby,” she said, directing him to a modest establishment called Tonic. The café was cozy and welcoming, its walls painted with vibrant leaves and vines. Niranjan ordered an espresso and a butter croissant, while Aleena opted for a filter coffee.

“You’ve changed,” she said, looking at him intently as they settled into a corner table.
“So have you,” he replied, though in his eyes, she still carried the same spark that had drawn him to her all those years ago.

Their conversation began tentatively, skirting around the years that had passed. Slowly, the walls of time dissolved. They talked about their children, their work, and the lives they had built since they last met. But beneath the surface, the weight of unsaid emotions lingered.

“Do you remember our junction?” Niranjan asked, his voice soft, almost wistful.
“How could I forget?” Aleena’s eyes glistened with emotion. “I knew you’d always be waiting there. It made me anxious if I didn’t see you, unless you’d told me beforehand.”

The memories flooded back—the narrow road where they’d exchanged secret notes, their hurried conversations hidden from prying eyes. Aleena’s confession was profound: “I burned all your letters before my marriage. I had no choice.”

Niranjan nodded, understanding. “How is he?” he asked, though the

words felt heavy on his tongue.
"He's a good man," she replied. "He's taken care of me and the kids well. But..." Her voice trailed off, leaving the rest unsaid. Niranjan didn't press her, sensing the complexity of her emotions.

The server brought their order, and Aleena eyed the croissant curiously.
"What is this?" she asked.

"A croissant. Try it," he said, breaking a piece for her.
She took a tentative bite, her eyes widening with surprise. "It's nice! This is the first time I've had this."
"We had a lot of firsts together," Niranjan said with a bittersweet smile.

Her cheeks flushed, and she looked away, blinking back tears. "Do you remember our late-night walks during the temple festivals?" she asked.
"The nights were beautiful," he replied, his voice thick with emotion. "Sometimes, when I look at the stars, I remember those moments."

They spent nearly an hour reminiscing, their words weaving joy with longing. When Niranjan finally asked for the bill, an air of finality settled between them.

He drove her back to where he'd picked her up earlier. She hesitated before getting out, turning to face him one last time.

"Niranjan," she began, her voice trembling. "I don't know if we'll meet again. But I want you to know something. I love you. Not as a wife or a girlfriend, but as a person. The memories we share are treasures I'll carry forever."

Tears welled up in his eyes. "Thank you," he whispered, his voice breaking.

She reached out, gently squeezing his hand before stepping out of the car. With one last lingering glance, she turned and walked away, her figure fading into the distance.

Niranjan sat there for a moment, allowing the emotions to wash over him. Wiping his tears, he started the car and drove on. The road sign ahead read: Salem, 125 kilometers.

Taking a deep breath, he pressed onward, the open highway stretching before him—a reminder of the journey still to come.

8

The Weight of Words

Poornima sat on the balcony of their new flat, the sprawling city glittered before her like a glittering tapestry. In her hand was a crumpled note, its edges damp from her restless grip. �Niranjan's words stared back at her:
"Going on a solo trip. May take some time. Unreachable. Need some time alone. Enough money in the bank."
The stark simplicity of the note belied its impact. It felt like a boulder dropped into the still waters of her life, sending ripples through everything she thought she understood about her husband.

They had been in a good place, hadn't they? Poornima's mind raced as she tried to make sense of it. Over the years, she had softened, her once insatiable need for status and material validation tempered by motherhood and time. But now, reading his note, a wave of regret washed over her. How much had he endured in silence? How much of his pain had she failed to see?

The memories rushed in, vivid and sharp. Their early days together had been filled with friction, especially with his mother, a traditional woman who saw Poornima's modern ways as defiance. The backhanded comments from Niranjan's relatives about her not wearing a mangalsutra, her disinterest in following the old customs, had felt like relentless jabs. In her frustration, Poornima had lashed out—not at them, but at Niranjan.

"Your cousins are awful people," she'd fumed after one particularly cutting remark at a family gathering.
"What can I do, Poornima?" he replied, exhaustion in his voice.
"They need to learn some manners!"
"I can't change them."

That helplessness had only enraged her more, and their fights grew frequent. On more than one occasion, she had stormed off to her parents' home, staying away for weeks at a stretch. It was always Niranjan who made the first move, apologizing even when he had nothing to apologize for. But she now realized that each time he did, a part of him had retreated further into himself.

When he had moved to Europe for a better job, she had refused to be with his family. "Not under your family's roof," she'd said firmly, insisting that she and Kriti stay with her parents instead. Niranjan had accepted her decision without protest, but now she wondered how deeply it had hurt him. The separation, both physical and emotional, had only widened the chasm between them.

Over time, her complaints had shifted focus. She'd begun to demand more—a bigger house, better clothes, a higher standard of living. Niranjan had worked tirelessly, juggling long hours and lonely nights, to fulfill her wishes. Yet, she had found reasons to criticize even his greatest efforts.

It was only after her Vipassana meditation retreat, ten days of enforced silence and introspection, that Poornima had begun to change. She'd returned with a restful mind, her sharp edges softened. Niranjan had noticed the difference immediately, though he never said much. Their arguments became fewer, their home a more peaceful place. But now, sitting on the balcony, she realized that his silence during those years hadn't been contentment—it had been resignation.

The note in her hand felt heavier than its weight. She looked at the dining table through the glass door, its three chairs mockingly empty. Kriti's eighteenth birthday had been meant to be a celebration, a milestone. Instead, it had been overshadowed by Niranjan's sudden departure. Her daughter had retreated into her own shell, the absence of her father casting a long shadow over her joy.

Poornima's gaze wandered back to the note. She traced the words with her finger, her vision blurring with unshed tears. Niranjan's voice echoed in her mind, words he'd often said but she had rarely heeded:�
"When you are healthy and wealthy, how you treat people will decide your future. We shouldn't use bad words and need to be kind, even if the other person isn't."

She used to brush off such remarks, thinking they were just his way of avoiding confrontation. But now, they struck her with the force of truth. Niranjan's actions had always reflected the values she had dismissed as passivity.

Poornima clutched the note tighter. She had spent so many years focusing on what she thought she lacked, blind to the sacrifices Niranjan had made to give her everything she wanted. And now, as she sat in the silence he had left behind, she realized the cost of her blindness.

The city lights flickered in the distance, their brilliance a cruel contrast to the emptiness she felt. She wiped her tears, staring out into the vastness. She didn't know where Niranjan was or when he'd return. But she knew one thing with certainty: when he did, she would be ready to listen—truly listen—for the first time in years.

9

The Space Between

The balcony door slid open with a faint whoosh, and Kriti tiptoed outside, her bare feet brushing against the cool tiles. The city shimmered in the fading light, its distant hum a constant reminder of life moving on. Her mother sat hunched in a corner, staring blankly at the skyline. The remnants of her eighteenth birthday decorations—a few limp balloons swaying in the gentle breeze—mocked the silence that enveloped their home.

Three days had passed since Niranjan's abrupt departure. Three days since her birthday celebration, carefully planned yet overshadowed by the cryptic note he left behind. Kriti had tried to smile for her friends, had tried to immerse herself in the fleeting joy of the occasion, but the words of the note lingered in her mind, heavy and incomprehensible.

Her mother's figure seemed smaller than usual, a shadow of the composed woman Kriti had always known. For the first time, she saw Poornima as something more than a stern parent—she saw vulnerability, raw and unguarded.

"Mom?" Kriti called softly.

Poornima turned, startled, her eyes betraying the weight she carried.

"Yes, Kriti?" she asked, her voice gentle but distant.

"Are you okay?" Kriti moved closer, sitting on the edge of the chair next to her.

Poornima gave a small, fleeting smile. "I'm fine, sweetheart. Just... thinking."

Kriti nodded, not pressing further. The silence between them was heavy with unuttered questions. Finally, she ventured, "Did he say anything to you before he left?"

Poornima shook her head. "Just the note. That's all."

Kriti's fingers ran on the balcony railing, her thoughts drifting. She had spent the past three days piecing together fragments of memory, trying to understand the man her father was. Her childhood had been a mosaic of moments—bright bursts of laughter and love interspersed with the tense silences of her parents' arguments. Niranjan had always been the stabilizer in their volatile household.

But now, she wondered what lay beneath that quiet. Had he been silently enduring all these years?

Fragments of memory

In her earliest recollections, her father was a distant figure. His phone calls from Europe crackled with static, their conversations brief and interrupted by time zones. The long, tearful goodbyes at airports had painted the backdrop of her childhood.

"Daddy is working abroad," her mother had explained. It was supposed to be temporary, yet the years stretched on, widening the gap between them.

When she was eight, he came home for good, and the distance between them began to shrink. Niranjan became her guide, her constant. He taught her to ride a bike, helped with her science projects, and sat patiently through her clumsy piano recitals. Poornima, once quick to anger, had softened over the years, and their home felt more like a haven. Yet, as she revisited those memories, Kriti realized how much of her father's warmth had been directed at her, and how little he and Poornima had truly connected.�

There were rare moments when Niranjan's mask slipped. She remembered catching him staring out of the window late at night, his silhouette framed by the soft glow of the streetlights. His face bore an expression she couldn't understand then. Now, she recognized it: exhaustion, perhaps even resignation.

The letter

Back in her room, Kriti unfolded the birthday letter Niranjan had written for her. His familiar slanted handwriting carried a warmth that made her throat tighten. She read the words again, lingering on the lines that felt like both advice and farewell:

"Eighteen. A milestone that marks the beginning of your journey into adulthood. A world of possibilities awaits you, filled with excitement, challenges, and everything in between.
The world can be a tumultuous place, Kriti. There will be moments of joy that touch the sky and moments of despair that sink you to your knees. Don't chase fleeting pleasures, for true happiness lies in finding peace within yourself.
Above all, Kriti, be kind. Kindness is not a weakness, but a strength. Be kind to yourself, forgive your mistakes, and learn from them. Be kind to others, for empathy and compassion are the cornerstones of a meaningful life."

Her hands trembled as she read the closing lines: "This journey I've embarked on is not just for myself, but for you too. I go to find the strength to face the storms within me, to become a better man, a better father for you. When I return, I hope to see a strong, independent woman who embraces life's challenges with the same grace and courage I see in you now. Remember, you are loved, Kriti. More than words can ever express."

The space between

Sitting with the letter in her lap, Kriti felt a wave of understanding wash over her. Her father's absence wasn't abandonment; it was a search for meaning, for healing. The spaces he had left—in their home, in their hearts—weren't voids. They were filled with his love, his hopes for them.

That evening, Kriti joined Poornima at the dining table. The silence between them felt lighter, less oppressive. They ate in solidarity, their bond subtly shifting, strengthened by the shared absence of the man who had tied them together. In his own way, Niranjan was teaching them both how to face the spaces he had left behind, and how to fill them with their own strength.

10

Echoes of Youth

The highway seemed endlessly with a ribbon of asphalt shimmering under the midday sun. The gentle hum of his car and the blur of passing landscapes lulled him into a state of reflection. Between Coimbatore and Salem, as he navigated familiar stretches of road, a fragment of his past flickered to life.

He had seen it again—a lone figure attempting to cross the highway, unsteady on his feet, oblivious to the speeding vehicles. Niranjan braked hard, his irritation bubbling briefly before being replaced by a wry smile. The recklessness of the man's actions mirrored his own youthful bravado, those restless days of daring and rebellion.

The memory came rushing back like a scene from a sepia-toned film. Niranjan was sixteen, eager to shed the innocence of boyhood and embrace the wild uncertainty of adolescence. Back then, the Bombay Bazaar junction in his village was the epicenter of youthful energy. Under the shade of a sprawling banyan tree, his seniors had established an art club that doubled as their unofficial headquarters.

It wasn't just an art club. It was a melting pot of ideas, friendships, and mischieves. The older boys planned cricket tournaments, debated politics, and, when the dusk ushered in, indulged in clandestine drinking sessions. For Niranjan and his gang, barely on the cusp of adulthood, these gatherings were tantalizingly out of reach.

The birth of "Pooja"

Niranjan and his closest friend, Sudheesh, were desperate to be part of the inner circle. Sudheesh, always the instigator, concocted a plan. "We'll call it a Pooja," he said, his eyes twinkling with mischief. "Tell everyone it's for Thekkele Shanmukhan's new job in Saudi. They'll never suspect a thing."

"Pooja? Seriously?" Niranjan laughed, skeptical but intrigued.
"Trust me," Sudheesh grinned. "Even if they find out, who's going to object to something holy?"

That evening, the plan unfolded with seamless precision. The boys gathered at their usual spot, armed with a bottle of toddy and snacks pilfered from a nearby shop. They sat under the banyan tree, their laughter muffled to avoid drawing unwanted attention. The "Pooja" became an instant legend among their peers, a code word for their secret gatherings.

The term caught on faster than anyone anticipated. Soon, "Poojas" were organized for every occasion—a new job, a wedding proposal, even a victorious cricket match. The art club was rebranded as "Illikalathappan Centre," a sly homage to a local deity. "Pooja for Illikalathappan" became shorthand for late-night revelries, each gathering laced with laughter, camaraderie, and the occasional reprimand from elders who remained blissfully unaware of the true nature of these "pious" celebrations.

The light and shadow of friendship - 1

Sudheesh had been the star of those days. With his quick wit and natural charm, he was the glue that held their ragtag group together. He was also the fastest bowler in their village cricket league. His fiery deliveries earned him admiration and envy in equal measures. But beneath his jovial facade lay a vulnerability that few noticed.

Years later, Sudheesh's life unraveled in ways Niranjan couldn't have imagined. A failed love affair had shattered his spirit, and his once-bright smile faded into a shadow of itself. The news of his suicide came on a gray morning, the weight of it settling heavily on Niranjan's chest. It was a cruel reminder of the fragility of the human spirit, of how even the most vibrant lives could be extinguished by the darkness within.

The light and shadow of friendship - 2

As Niranjan steered his car through the bends of the highway, he found himself thinking of Sudheesh's laugh, the way it had lit up even their dullest days. He thought of the banyan tree, the stolen moments of joy and mischief, and the lessons those youthful escapades had taught him.

He realized now that their so-called "Poojas" had been more than just rebellious acts. They were expressions of freedom, experiments in pushing boundaries and finding meaning in a world that often felt stifling. But freedom, he knew now, came with a cost—a responsibility to oneself and others.

The signboard ahead read Salem, 90 kilometers. Niranjan adjusted his grip on the steering wheel, his mind settling into a resolve. The memories of his youth, tinged with both joy and sorrow, were not just echoes of the past. They were part of the mosaic of his life, fragments that shaped the man he was becoming.

As the car sped forward, the sun immersed in the sky, casting long shadows on the road ahead. The journey was far from over, but somehow, Niranjan felt a sense of clarity. The road stretched endlessly before him, inviting him to continue—to reflect, to heal, and to rediscover the pieces of himself he had long forgotten.

11

Konchum Mainakkale

The hills were beginning to flatten out as the road curved towards the plains. Salem was now a memory in the rearview mirror. The music in the car was mellow, the kind that fit journeys like this—quiet, unhurried, and inward-looking. The kind that gave you permission to think, and sometimes, to feel.
"Konchum Mainakkale..."

That song. Niranjan had heard it hundreds of times, but it never aged. A playful melody from his youth, filled with childlike innocence and a strange power to gently lift him out of any mood he found himself trapped in. Grief. Doubt. Loneliness. Even now, as he drove alone on a stretch between Salem and Bengaluru, that voice, that tune—it loosened something inside him. It always did.

The road rose briefly, leading to an overbridge. As he took the left turn down towards the Bengaluru highway, he eased the car slowly onto the main road. It was the kind of cautious drive that invites unexpected moments. And there it was.

A TVS moped. The kind you'd find in every other household across the Tamil Nadu countryside. Modest. Dependable. On it, a man—probably in his fifties—and behind him, a girl, not more than twenty, her dupatta fluttering faintly in the breeze. There was something striking about her—not in the usual sense of beauty, but something honest, unfiltered, real.

She looked at him as their vehicles came side by side in slow motion. Niranjan smiled without thinking. A simple smile. The kind that says, *I see you.*
And she smiled back. Briefly. Softly. Her eyes stayed on him a moment longer than necessary, and just before the car pulled ahead, he noticed—the metal glint of crutches resting on her lap. Her left leg was missing below the knee.

His smile lingered. It wasn't pity. It wasn't shock. It was something else. Recognition, maybe. Of the kind of strength that comes disguised.

Her father noticed the smile. Protective eyes met Niranjan's in the rearview mirror. There was no smile returned. Just a quiet, unsaid *watch yourself.*

A few kilometers later, the road opened into a small dusty clearing where a T-shop stood with a few plastic chairs, a rusted table, and the smell of boiling ginger tea mixing with fried vadai. Niranjan pulled over. He didn't need tea. Not really. But he often stopped at places like these. It wasn't about the chai—it was the rhythm of the place, the sound of conversations, the microcosm of life in each stop. He liked overhearing things. It made him feel connected to the world he mostly drifted away from.

A group of young men were mid-argument over the latest Thala Ajith film.
"Bro, acting-la mass illa, mass-aa life da!"
"Come on da, Vijay thaan real beast da!"

He smiled as he sipped the tea. Tamil cinema had its own religion, and here, the roadside shop was a temple. The debates weren't about logic—they were about loyalty. Passion. Homegrown drama.

Moments later, the familiar sputter of a two-wheeler came into earshot. The same TVS moped pulled in. The man parked it carefully, stepping off and gently helping his daughter get down. She held onto his shoulder, balancing as she reached for her crutches.

Niranjan stood, still holding his paper cup, and nodded.
"*Enga poguringa, anna?*" he asked with a polite smile.

The man looked up, surprised, but not unfriendly. "*Avluku bike la suthanumnu pidikkum. Avalukku kaal kashtam irundhaalum, naan appa illaya? Konjam konjam edam ellam kaamikarom.*" (She loves traveling by bike. Even though she has leg difficulties... I'm her father, right? I take her around wherever I can.)

The girl smiled again. This time it was a little more open. Her eyes had the calm of someone who had made peace with pain and decided to smile anyway.

Niranjan asked her, "*Oru chance kedaicha, neenga enga poganum nu aasai?*" (If you got a chance, where would you go?)

She looked at him as if she had rehearsed that answer all her life.
"*Kashmir.*" she said. Simply. Like saying *home*.
The air went still for a moment. The only sound was a radio playing in the shop—some old Ilaiyaraaja tune floating through the dusty wind.

They spoke for a while—nothing too deep, just enough to share a corner of their lives with each other. Before leaving, Niranjan turned to her father and said, "*Neenga romba periya appa sir.*" (You're a wonderful father, sir.)
The man didn't reply immediately, but his eyes softened. There was a

lifetime of stories behind that nod.

Back on the highway, the sun was leaning westward. The road to Bengaluru stretched ahead, dotted with trucks and buses and memories. Inside the car, the music shifted again.
"Vazhve vazhvavarkku..."

The lyrics struck him differently now. Life belongs to those who live it—fully, with scars, with stumbles, and with the will to smile anyway. Niranjan let out a small laugh, somewhere between joy and ache.

Somewhere between Salem and Bengaluru, between a song and a stranger's story, a little part of him felt lighter.

12

The City of Contrasts

Bengaluru had always been a paradox to Niranjan. Its sprawling IT parks stood alongside bustling markets where the present seemed reluctant to let go of the past. Here, grand skyscrapers towered over modest, crumbling houses. The rhythmic whir of software development coexisted with the timeless chants of street-side vendors selling jasmine garlands and piping hot masala dosas. The city of contrast, it is.

For Niranjan, Bengaluru had been both a refuge and a crucible. It was the city where he had escaped the suffocating tension of his life with Poornima. The vibrancy of the city offered him a temporary solace, a space to blend into the crowd and lose himself in its ceaseless energy. Yet, even amidst the chaos, the shadows of his troubled marriage followed him relentlessly.

A routine to escape

Every evening, after work, Niranjan would visit the Sri Ramakrishna Ashram nestled near the Ulsoor Lake. The ashram was his sanctuary, its tranquil ambiance a stark contrast to the hustle and noise of the city. Here, under the watchful gaze of Swami Vivekananda's statue, he would sit cross-legged and meditate. The hours before the Sandhya Aarti became his escape, his moments of silence amidst a life that felt perpetually loud.

He rarely stayed for the discourses, leaving the premises before the speakers began. Words, he thought, were insufficient. Experience was what he sought—a connection that transcended verbal expression.

One evening, after his meditation, an old man approached him. Clad in simple robes and radiating a pacific energy, the man waited patiently as Niranjan gathered his belongings.
"Keep doing it," the old man said, his voice soft yet imbued with a certain gravity. "You will reach there. We will meet again."

Niranjan looked up, startled. Before he could respond, the man had vanished into the crowd. The words lingered with him long after, a cryptic message that felt like both a reassurance and a riddle.

The tensions at home

Even in Bengaluru, Poornima's possessiveness managed to intrude. Every phone call from a female colleague or a friend became a cause for suspicion. Poornima's accusations were exhausting. Her constant surveillance turned his phone into a dreadful device.

A city of contradictions

Bengaluru's duality mirrored Niranjan's own inner conflict. The city's glass-fronted tech parks symbolized progress, ambition, and the pursuit of success, while the narrow lanes of Shivajinagar reminded him of life's simpler, more grounded pleasures. He often found himself drawn to these older parts of the city—to the aroma of roasted coffee, the clang of temple bells, and the cheerful banter of shopkeepers who knew their customers by name.

He struck up conversations with the city's street vendors, whose resilience and warmth left an impression on him. An old bookseller near MG Road had once told him, "Saar, every story has its reader. Some books wait decades before finding theirs. Perhaps people are the same."

Those words stayed with him. Niranjan began to see Bengaluru not just as a city of opportunities, but as a living, breathing entity—one that embraced contradictions without judgment.

A revelation

As days turned into months, Niranjan began to see his relationship with Poornima through a new lens. Her accusations weren't just about him; they stemmed from her own insecurities, her fear of abandonment. Similarly, his silence wasn't just a coping mechanism—it was a symptom of his growing detachment, a rebellion against a life he felt trapped in.

One evening, as he sat by Ulsoor Lake, watching the ripples spread across the water, a realization settled over him. He wasn't running from his problems; he was seeking a way to understand them. Bengaluru, with its relentless energy and still harbors, had given him the space to reflect, to detangle the knots within himself.

Moving forward

Niranjan's time in Bengaluru was a turning point. It wasn't a place of answers, but a city that had posed the right questions. As he prepared to leave for the next leg of his journey, he felt a strange sense of gratitude—for the city, for its people, and even for the challenges it had presented.

The road ahead was uncertain, but Bengaluru had taught him to embrace the conundrum—in the world and within himself. As he drove out of the city, the towering skyline receding in his rearview mirror, Niranjan felt lighter, as if he had left behind not just a city, but a part of his past that no longer defined him.

13

Morality Tested

The road from Bengaluru to Varanasi was a long and winding one, cutting through the diverse landscapes of Telangana and Maharashtra before reaching the holy city. Each stretch of highway brought Niranjan closer to his destination and deeper into his thoughts. The solitude of the drive gave him ample time to reflect on the choices he had made, the trials he had endured, and the man he had become.

As the car hummed along a stretch of road just past Hyderabad, Niranjan's mind drifted to a moment he had long buried. It had been one of the darkest chapters of his life, a time when Poornima's aggression had pushed him to the edge of his values. The relentless accusations, the constant surveillance, the suffocating atmosphere at home—they had driven him to a place he never thought he'd visit.

The encounter

It had been a stormy evening in Bengaluru. The skies were heavy with clouds, mirroring the weight in Niranjan's heart. After yet another explosive argument with Poornima, he stormed out of the house, the anger and frustration boiling over. He drove aimlessly, his mind riled up with resentment and exhaustion, until he found himself in a part of the city he didn't recognize.

The neon sign outside a dingy building caught his eye: a garish, flickering symbol of a world he had never dared to step into. Without thinking, he parked the car and walked inside, his feet moving almost of their own accord. The dimly lit interior smelled of cheap perfume and desperation. A woman approached him, her smile forced and weary, her eyes betraying a life lived in shadows.

"Looking for company?" she asked, her voice soft but tired.

Niranjan hesitated, his resolve faltering. He had come here in a moment of weakness, driven by the desire to rebel against the constraints of his life. But as he looked at the woman, he saw not temptation, but a person—a human being with her own story, her own struggles.

"What's your name?" he asked, surprising even himself.

The woman raised an eyebrow, wary of his tone. "Does it matter?" she replied.

"It does," Niranjan said earnestly. "I'm not here for... that. I just... I need to talk."

A story shared

Her name was Shanti. She was from a small village in Andhra Pradesh, lured to the city with promises of a better life that had quickly turned into a nightmare. Her husband had abandoned her, and with no family to fall back on, she had turned to this work out of desperation.

As she spoke, Niranjan listened intently, the anger and frustration within him ebbing away. Her words were a mirror, reflecting his own struggles in a different light. The pressures of survival, the compromises made for loved ones, the resilience in the face of unimaginable hardships—these were threads that wove their lives together, no matter how different they seemed on the surface.

By the time Shanti finished her story, Niranjan felt a deep sense of shame—not for being there, but for how close he had come to betraying his own principles. He reached into his wallet, pulled out a few crisp notes, and placed them on the table.

"Take this," he said, his voice steady. "Not for… anything. Just for you. For whatever you need."

Shanti looked at him, her expression a mix of gratitude and disbelief. "You're a strange man," she said with a faint smile tugging at her lips. Niranjan nodded, his own smile tinged with sadness. "Maybe. Or maybe I'm just trying to figure out who I am."

Reflections on the road

As the memory faded, Niranjan's hands tightened on the steering wheel. That night had been a turning point for him, a moment when he had come face-to-face with the person he never wanted to become. Despite the pressures, despite the pain, he had chosen to hold on to his values, to remain true to himself.

As he drove away, the landscape began to change. The dense greenery of Telangana gave way to the sprawling plains of Maharashtra, dotted with farms and small villages. The journey was long, but Niranjan felt lighter with every mile, as if shedding the weight of his past with each passing kilometer.

Passing through Nagpur, the orange capital of India, Niranjan stopped at a roadside stall for a quick break. The vendor, an elderly man with a kind smile, handed him a glass of fresh orange juice. Niranjan struck up a conversation, learning about the man's family, his struggles, and his dreams for his grandchildren. These small exchanges reminded Niranjan of the interconnectedness of human lives, the shared experiences that bound people together despite their differences.

The road to Varanasi stretched ahead, winding through the heart of India. It wasn't just a physical journey anymore; it was a journey within, a quest to reconcile the man he had been with the man he wanted to become.

The resolve

As dusk fell, Niranjan pulled over by a stretch of road to rest. The horizon burned orange, giving way to a purple twilight. He stepped out, stretching his legs and breathing in the cool air. The scent of earth after a brief drizzle reminded him of home, of Kriti's laughter, and even of Poornima's sharp words—now distant echoes in his mind.

Niranjan closed his eyes, letting the hum of the world around him blend with the silence within. The journey was long, yet, he began to feel the stirrings of peace—a resolve to face whatever lay ahead with the same unyielding strength that had carried him this far.

14

A Silent Battle

The days had turned into weeks, and Poornima's restlessness had grown into a tangible weight that hung over the flat. The usually lively home felt suffocating in Niranjan's absence. Her once-distracted energy had shifted; now, she lingered at the dining table, staring at the untouched food, or stood by the window, watching the city lights flicker.

Kriti, too, had noticed the change in her mother. Poornima had always been a force of nature in her life—sharp-tongued, confident, and relentlessly focused on appearances. But now, she seemed smaller, almost fragile, as though Niranjan's absence had unraveled something deep within her.

An uneasy routine

Poornima tried to maintain an air of normalcy. She still went to her yoga classes, attended the occasional kitty parties. But the effort was forced, her smiles brittle and her conversations shallow. Her friends noticed, but Poornima waved off their concerns with vague reassurances.

At home, she avoided Kriti's questions, retreating into silence when her daughter tried to ask about her father. "He'll come back," she'd say, her voice thin with an uncertainty she didn't want to acknowledge.

One evening, as Poornima prepared dinner, Kriti entered the kitchen. She leaned against the counter, watching her mother chop vegetables with mechanical precision.
"You're worried about him," Kriti said softly.
Poornima paused, the knife still in her hand. "Of course I'm worried. He's your father."
"I mean... really worried," Kriti pressed. "Like you're afraid he won't come back."

Poornima's shoulders slumped. For a moment, she looked like she might cry, but she took a deep breath and steadied herself. "He needs this, Kriti. I... I've been thinking a lot about how things have been between us. How I... pushed him."
Kriti's brow furrowed. "What do you mean?"
Poornima set the knife down and turned to face her daughter. "Your father is a good man. Better than I deserve, sometimes. And I... I didn't make it easy for him. I was... angry a lot. At him, at life. I wanted more. Always more."

Kriti watched her mother carefully, sensing the vulnerability behind her words. "But he never complained. At least not to me," Kriti said.

Poornima smiled faintly. "That's who he is. He doesn't say much, but he... feels deeply. I think I took that for granted."

The weight of reflection

After dinner, Poornima sat on the balcony, staring out at the city. The note Niranjan had left was folded neatly in her lap, its edges worn from being unfolded and refolded too many times. She read it again, though she already knew every word by heart:

"Going on a solo trip. May take some time. Unreachable. Need some time alone. Enough money in the bank."

The starkness of the words cut through her every time. Niranjan's detachment was almost maddening. How could he leave so simply, so completely, after everything they had built together?

But then she thought about the years leading up to this moment. The fights. The accusations. Her relentless need to control every aspect of their lives. Poornima had been so focused on shaping their future that she had ignored the cracks forming in the present.

Niranjan had endured so much in silence, his patience stretching thin as he tried to hold their family together.

Now, as she sat there, she realized how blind she had been to his struggles. She had assumed his strength would always carry them, never considering the toll it might take on him.

A step forward

The following morning, Poornima woke early and found herself scrolling through old photos on her phone. Images of family vacations, Kriti's school events, warm moments at home. Niranjan was in most of them, his presence, the anchor in their chaotic lives.

She paused on a picture from their trip to Ooty years ago. They had stayed at a quaint homestay, and Niranjan had spent hours teaching Kriti how to fly a kite in the open field behind the house. Poornima remembered how he had laughed that day, a genuine, carefree laugh she hadn't heard in years. The memory brought a lump to her throat. She realized then that she didn't just miss Niranjan. She missed the man he had been before their lives had become so complicated, so heavy with unspoken grievances.

Poornima took a deep breath and made a decision. She would start therapy, something Niranjan had gently suggested years ago but she had dismissed outright. Maybe it was too late to undo the damage, but it wasn't too late to change herself—for Kriti, for Niranjan, and most importantly, for herself.

The realization

That evening, as she sat with Kriti on the couch, Poornima finally broke her silence. "I've decided to see someone. A therapist."

Kriti looked up, surprised but relieved. "That's... that's a good idea, Mom."

Poornima nodded, her gaze steady. "I think it's time I started dealing with things. For your father. For us."

Kriti reached out and took her mother's hand, giving it a gentle squeeze. In that moment, the tension between them began to ease, replaced by an unstated understanding.

As they sat there, the city buzzing softly in the background, Poornima felt the faintest stirrings of hope. Niranjan's absence was still a gaping void in their lives, but somehow, she felt like she was taking a step toward bridging the distance—not just between herself and him, but within her own heart.

15

Father's Love story

Kriti strolled along the sandy beach, her bare feet sinking into the cool grains as the waves lapped gently against the shore. Beside her walked Niranjan, his pace steady and calm, a presence she had grown to lean on. The sun hung low on the horizon, painting the sky in hues of orange and pink, as if nature itself had conspired to set the stage for the conversation that was about to unfold.

Niranjan, sensing his daughter's turmoil, decided it was time to share a piece of himself she had never known.

"Kriti," he began, his voice emitting both hesitation and resolve, "I want to tell you something. Something I've kept to myself for years."
Kriti turned to him, curiosity flickering in her eyes. "What is it, Dad?"

He took a deep breath, the salty sea air filling his lungs. "When I was young, I fell in love. Deeply. With a girl from our village."
Her eyebrows shot up in surprise. "You did? You never told me that!"

A faint smile played on Niranjan's lips, one tinted with nostalgia. "There's a lot I haven't told you. But now... I think it's time you knew."

Aleena

He began to recount the story of Aleena, a girl with laughter like wind chimes and eyes that spoke of dreams beyond their little village. Niranjan's love for her had been all-encompassing, a heady mix of youthful passion and idealism. Their stolen glances across the schoolyard, the secret notes exchanged on narrow paths, and their whispered conversations by the banyan tree—these were the memories he had carried with him all his life.

"She was... extraordinary," he said, his voice soft. "She had this way of seeing the world that made you believe anything was possible. But life wasn't easy for her. She came from a conservative family, and the idea of us being together... it wasn't something they could accept."

Kriti listened intently, her heart aching for the young man her father had been, and for the love that had slipped through his fingers.

"What happened?" she asked gently.

"We tried," Niranjan said, a wistful smile on his face. "We tried to make it work. But there were too many obstacles, too many people who thought they knew what was best for us. In the end, Aleena chose her family's honor over our love. And I... I chose to let her go."

A connection across time

Kriti's thoughts drifted to her own recent heartbreak, the boy she had loved and lost. She saw her own struggles mirrored in her father's story, and for the first time, she understood the depth of his empathy.

"Did you ever stop loving her?" she asked, her voice barely above a whisper.

Niranjan paused, his gaze fixed on the horizon. "I think... a part of me will always carry her with me. But love changes over time. It becomes less about holding on and more about letting go. And in letting go, I found something greater. I found your mother. And I found you."

Kriti's eyes welled up, and she looked away, blinking back tears. "Do you think... do you think love is worth the pain?"

Niranjan stopped walking, turning to face her. "Yes," he said simply. "Love is always worth it. Even when it hurts. Because it teaches you something about yourself. It makes you stronger. Wiser. It's a part of what makes us human."

A new understanding

As they resumed their walk, Kriti felt a new sense of connection to her father. His story, shared so openly, had given her a glimpse into the man behind the parent. She saw his strength, not in his stoicism, but in his vulnerability. In his willingness to love, to lose, and to carry on.
"Thank you for telling me," she responded. "It helps. It really does."

Niranjan placed a reassuring hand on her shoulder. "You're stronger than you think, Kriti. And no matter what happens, you'll come out of this better than before. I'm proud of you. Always."

They continued walking as the waves carried away their footprints. In the fading light, Kriti felt a sense of peace she hadn't known in weeks. Her father's story had reminded her of the resilience of love—not just the romantic kind, but the love that binds families together, even in the face of loss and uncertainty.

16

Clarity

Kriti sat by the window of her room, staring out at the city lights as though staring at infinity. The conversation with her father earlier on the beach lingered in her mind, replaying like a cherished melody. Her father's story had stirred something deep within her, a mix of empathy, awe, and an aching understanding.

Growing up, Niranjan had always been her protector. He was the one who guided her gently through life, his wisdom and composure balancing out Poornima's intensity. But she realized now that she had never truly seen him—not the man behind the father. His vulnerability, his strength, and the weight he had carried for so many years had been hidden behind his smiles and unwavering patience.

Childhood memories

Her earliest memories of him were a kaleidoscope of small moments: the way he'd tuck her in at night with a story, his steady hand holding hers as they crossed a busy street, the way he'd sit through her piano recitals, clapping the loudest even when she faltered. He was her constant, her anchor in a world that often felt overwhelming.

But as she grew older, she began to notice the cracks. The tension between her parents was palpable, even if they tried to shield her from it. Niranjan's silences grew heavier, and his smiles seemed harder to come by. She remembered how he'd retreat to his study after dinner, the faint hum of his favorite instrumental music filtering through the door. At the time, she thought he just enjoyed solitude. Now, she understood it was his way of coping.

The weight he carried

The story of Aleena had been a revelation, but it was more than just a tale of youthful love. It was a window into Niranjan's soul, a glimpse of the man who had endured so much yet never wavered in his love for his family. Kriti couldn't help but think of her own recent heartbreak, the pain of losing someone she had cared for deeply. It was a pain she had thought would consume her, but now she saw it differently.

Her father had carried the weight of loss and heartbreak, yet emerged stronger, choosing to build a life with Poornima and raise a family. His resilience gave her hope, a reminder that pain was not an end but a passage.

Kriti's thoughts turned to Poornima. Her mother had always been a dominant force in their lives, her sharp words and unrelenting expectations shaping much of Kriti's childhood. But even Poornima, with all her fire, had begun to change. Her decision to start therapy was a step Kriti hadn't expected, a sign that her mother was beginning to confront her own demons. For the first time, Kriti saw her parents as more than just authoritative figures; they were individuals, flawed and beautiful in their humanity.

A newfound clarity

As the night deepened, Kriti picked up her father's letter again. She had

read it countless times, but the words never lost their impact:
"Above all, Kriti, be kind. Kindness is not a weakness, but a strength. Be kind to yourself, forgive your mistakes, and learn from them. Be kind to others, for empathy and compassion are the cornerstones of a meaningful life."

Those words resonated now more than ever. Kriti realized that her father's greatest lesson wasn't in the advice he gave but in the life he lived. He had shown her what it meant to be resilient, to love unconditionally, and to find strength in vulnerability.

The bond reimagined

The next morning, as Kriti and Poornima shared a quiet breakfast, Kriti felt a shift in their dynamic. Her mother seemed lighter, the usual sharpness in her tone replaced by something softer, almost hesitant.

"Mom," Kriti began, setting her mug of tea down. "I think Dad... he's given us more than we've realized. Maybe it's time we give something back."

Poornima looked up, her expression unreadable at first. Then, slowly, she nodded. "I've been thinking about that," she said. "I don't know if we can ever make up for what he's endured, but... we can try."

It wasn't a perfect resolution, but it was a start. And as Kriti left for her room, she felt a sense of peace she hadn't felt in a long time. Her father's journey was still unfolding, but in his absence, he had brought their family closer. He had given them the courage to face their own truths, to mend the fractures they had ignored for too long.

Kriti sat by the window again, watching the sun rise over the city. In her heart, she carried her father's lessons, his love, and his unwavering belief in the power of kindness. She resolved to hold on to those lessons, not just for herself, but for him—the man who had always been her anchor, her guide, and her greatest teacher.

17

A Journey Within

The road to Varanasi spanned like an unbroken thread weaving through the fabric of India. The car's murmur became a backdrop to Niranjan's thoughts, a rhythmic companion to his reflections. Telangana had given way to the sprawling plains of Maharashtra, and now, the heartland of Uttar Pradesh loomed closer. Each passing kilometer brought him nearer to his destination, and yet, he knew the true journey was unfolding within him.

Arriving in Varanasi

As Niranjan neared Varanasi, the landscape began to change. The fields gave way to narrow lanes crowded with rickshaws, motorbikes, and an endless sea of humanity. The city's energy was palpable, a chaotic symphony of sights, sounds, and smells. Temples stood side by side with bustling markets, and the sacred Ganges flowed through it all, tranquil and unyielding.

Varanasi, where life and death coexisted in harmony. Niranjan had read about the ghats—those ancient steps leading down to the river—but seeing them in person was overwhelming. The Dashashwamedh Ghat was alive with activity, priests performing rituals, devotees offering prayers, and tourists capturing the moment through their lenses. Yet, amid the chaos, there was an inexplicable stillness, as though the city itself breathed in a rhythm only it understood.

The sannyasis and the aghoris

Niranjan found himself drawn to the ghats where the sannyasins meditated, their ochre robes blending with the earthy tones of the steps. He observed them from a distance, admiring their discipline, their commitment to a life of simplicity and spiritual pursuit. Some welcomed his curiosity, sharing their wisdom in measured words, while others remained enigmatic, their silence a language of its own.

But it was the Aghoris who left an indelible impression on him. Clad in ashes, their dreadlocks cascading down their backs, they were a stark contrast to the serene sannyasins. Niranjan watched as one of them performed a ritual by the river, a hauntingly beautiful act that seemed to transcend the boundaries of life and death. Despite their fearsome appearance, there was a profound depth to their philosophy, a reminder that the sacred and the profane were two sides of the same coin.

A meeting with the past

One evening, after a long walk along the ghats, Niranjan returned to his modest guesthouse. The air was heavy with the scent of incense and the distant rendition of evening aarti. As he entered the courtyard, he noticed a figure waiting for him, seated on a stone bench under a flickering lantern.

It was the old man he had met years ago at the Sri Ramakrishna Ashram in Bengaluru.
Niranjan's breath caught in his throat. The man's face was etched with time, but his eyes held the same calm intensity.

"We'll meet again," the man said cryptically, his voice steady, as though

this meeting was a precursor to something greater.
"I told you we'd meet again," the man said.

They exchanged a few words, the old man's insights brief but profound. Niranjan left the encounter with a sense of curiosity and anticipation, feeling as though the man's promise of meeting again held a deeper significance.

A night of reflection

That night, Niranjan sat by the river, the Ganges shimmering under the moonlight. He thought about his journey, the people he had met, and the lessons he had learned. He thought about Poornima and Kriti, about the love he had carried and the mistakes he had made. And for the first time in years, he felt whole

Varanasi had embraced him, not as a tourist or an outsider, but as a seeker. The city's energy had seeped into him, its timeless wisdom reminding him that life was not a series of destinations but a journey within.

As the first light of dawn touched the horizon, Niranjan closed his eyes and whispered a prayer, not for himself, but for those he loved. And in that moment, he felt the stirrings of a peace he had long sought, a peace that promised to stay with him, no matter where the road led next.

18

The Final Smile

Twenty-one days in Varanasi had transformed Niranjan. The city had enveloped him, folding him into its tapestry of rituals, chaos, and serenity. Each day had been a meditation, each moment a lesson. The ghats, the sannyasins, the incessant chant of prayers—they had all become part of his life.

The mornings began with a walk along the riverbanks. Niranjan had grown fond of the chai vendor at Assi Ghat, a wiry man with a toothy grin who would serve him tea in clay cups.

"Good morning, Banarasi," the man would call him, a nickname that had stuck among the locals. It was their way of accepting him, a sign that he was no longer a visitor but one of their own.

The evenings were his time of solitude. He'd sit by the Ganges, watching the city shift into its nightly rhythm. The ghats would glow with the light of a hundred diyas, their flames floating gently on the water. He'd listen to the aarti, its chants resonating deep within him, as though the river itself was singing.

The unexpected encounter

On his twenty-first day in Varanasi, Niranjan set out for his evening walk, the city bustling around him. As he neared a ghat, he saw a familiar figure sitting on the steps. His heart skipped a beat. It was the old man he had met years ago at the Sri Ramakrishna Ashram in Bengaluru.

The old man's eyes twinkled with recognition. "You've come far," he said, gesturing for Niranjan to sit beside him.�

They spoke for hours, their conversation weaving through topics of existence, spirituality, and the inevitability of life's end. Niranjan felt a profound sense of clarity as the man spoke, his words like a key unlocking doors within Niranjan's heart.

The final night

Back in his room at the modest guesthouse, Niranjan prepared for bed. The room was simple, adorned with little more than a cot, a wooden desk, and an oil lamp that cast flickering shadows on the walls. On the desk lay his journal, its pages filled with reflections from his journey, and a worn copy of the Kathopanishad, a philosophical text he had carried with him throughout his travels.

He opened the book, its pages marked with notes and underlined passages.
One line stood out:
"The self cannot be known through words or intellect. It can only be experienced by the one who seeks within."

As he read the words, Niranjan felt a deep sense of contentment. He lay back on the cot, his eyes closing as a faint smile curved his lips. The sounds of the city filtered into the room—the distant chanting, the rustle of leaves in the breeze, the occasional bark of a stray dog. They lulled him into a peaceful sleep.

The morning revelation

When the hotel staff knocked on Niranjan's door the next morning, there was no answer. Concerned, they entered the room and found him lying on the cot, his face serene, his smile still intact. He had passed away in his sleep, his journey completed not in the city of Varanasi, but within himself.

The staff, saddened yet awed by the tranquility of his passing, found a piece of paper on the desk. It was addressed to Poornima and Kriti.
The words were few but profound:
"Life is fleeting, like the flame of a diya. But its light, if shared with love, lives on. Remember, I have always loved you both."

The journey home

The guesthouse staff contacted Poornima and Kriti using the address found in Niranjan's wallet. The news reached them with the weight of a thunderclap, shattering the resolve they had begun to build in his absence. Poornima held the letter to her chest, tears streaming down her face, while Kriti sat silently, her hands trembling as she clutched her father's journal.

When they arrived in Varanasi to perform his last rites, they were met by a community that spoke of Niranjan with reverence. The chai vendor, the guesthouse staff, the sannyasins at the ghats—all had stories to share of the man who had embraced their city and their lives. He had left an indelible mark, not through grand gestures, but through simple acts of kindness and genuine connection.

As Poornima and Kriti released his ashes into the Ganges, they felt a strange sense of peace. The river, timeless and eternal, carried him away, but his love and lessons remained with them.

Varanasi had given Niranjan his final resting place, but it had also given his family a new beginning. In his death, he had shown them the path to healing, to understanding, and to finding their own journeys within.

Sijeesh, a seasoned creative director, has spent years crafting compelling visual experiences — but the written word has always been his first love. A published poet, short story writer, and chronicler of journeys in various magazines and anthologies, *The Journey Within* marks his debut as a novelist.

Cover design & Illustratiions
Sudheesh Pellissery

Editor: Arpita Talukdar

Thanks: Abhilash Ramachandran, Binu Sivam, Binu K S, Dhanya Ravi, Edwin David Sam, Gireesh Kumar, Jagannath, Jithin C J, Madhu Karuthedath, Mejo Kuriachan, Prasad P S, Praveen Vattamparambath, Rehna Haridas, Rudranath, Satarupa chakravarty, Shaliny Chandy, Sharan, Sheena, Thomas Shine, Varsha

9 789334 193091

Printed at Repro India Ltd.